TERROR ON THE TRAINING GROUND

KEITH BRUMPTON

Dedicated to Annabelle Loftus

First published in 2010 by Usborne Publishing Ltd., Usborne House,
83-85 Saffron Hill, London EC1N 8RT, England.
www.usborne.com

A CIP catalogue record for this book is available from the British Library.

J MAMJJASOND/10 95831 ISBN 9781409504832
Printed in Reading, Berkshire, UK.

DINO FC

Dear Dino-soccer fan,

My name is Terry Triceratops and regular fans will know me as the team's fullback. But now I've been requested by our chairman to take over as player-manager.

I know the team has had some bad results recently (well every season actually) but I'm still convinced we can climb away from the bottom of the table. I'll be giving it 100%, so I hope I can count on your support!

All the best

Terry Triceratops

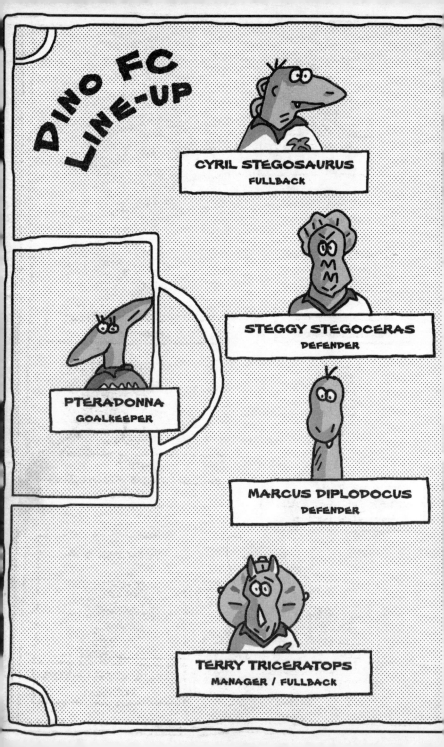

ARCHIE OPTERYX
LEFT WINGER

ALBERT ALLOSAURUS
CENTRE MIDFIELD

CELIA COELOPHYSIS
FORWARD

GWEN CORYTHOSAURUS
CENTRE MIDFIELD

JOSÉ HETERODONTOSAURUS
FORWARD

ERIC ALLOSAURUS
RIGHT MIDFIELD

TODAY'S SUB:

OLLIE OVIRAPTOR
FORWARD

Terry Triceratops was young and he was keen, but right now he was feeling like a pterodactyl in an ocean – out of his depth. He hadn't asked to be manager of Dino FC, the worst team in the Dinosaur Premier League, it just sort of happened...

First the team lost almost every match that season. Then their old manager resigned, saying he would rather dance on hot molten rocks than be in charge of such a useless rabble. And finally the club chairman, Danny Deinonychus, had come to Terry.

I'D LIKE YOU TO BE MANAGER UNTIL I CAN FIND SOMEONE BETTER...

Now Terry was in charge of the team, he was really enjoying it. But he was under a lot of pressure. Since he had taken over as manager, the team had lost three more matches and now it was crunch time. Relegation to League Two was on the cards.

Terry and the team knew they would have to find a win from somewhere. The question was...where?!

Dino FC's next match was against AFC Fossil. Even their most loyal fans didn't think they'd win.

Martin Millipede
season ticket holder ↘

I HATE TO SAY IT BUT WE'RE FOR THE DROP!

And up in the TV tower, the experts from the DBC (the Dinosaur Broadcasting Corporation) were feeling gloomy about their chances too.

SLIM CHANCE.

NO CHANCE.

In the team's dressing cave it was chaos.

By the time they found Marcus Diplodocus's sock (in his bag), there was no time for Terry to give his prematch tactics talk. He was disappointed, because there was a lot he'd wanted to say about "team spirit" and "not letting the fans down". But now that would have to wait until half-time.

The referee darted into their cave. He was a small ichthyostega.

"Hey, I'm not a lad," sniffed Celia Coelophysis, Dino FC's speedy forward. The referee looked embarrassed and told them they had two minutes until kick-off.

"Okay, team," said Terry, forced to shorten his talk to just a few words...

He was interrupted by Steggy
Stegoceras, the squad's grumpy defender.

Terry sighed. He sometimes wished
Steggy would keep his unhelpful thoughts to
himself.

Terry tried again to raise the team's
spirits. "Come on, we can do this. Let's get
out there and get ourselves a result!"

Everyone nodded, but then Eric and Albert Allosaurus started squabbling over who should be first out of the dressing cave.

Eric and Albert were twins and they were always fighting.

In the end, it was Terry who led the side out onto the pitch. As the team ran out, the long grass rippled in the gentle breeze of a prehistoric summer's evening. Terry was feeling really nervous now. They needed the points so badly. How would the team play?

Terry looked up and saw the club's chairman, Danny Deinonychus, taking his seat. He didn't look very happy. Terry knew that Danny was already talking to other possible managers about taking over at Dino FC.

But there was no time to worry about that now as the game was about to begin.

CHAPTER 2

The match went well for the first ten seconds or so. But then Dino FC's flying goalie, Pteradonna, collided with fullback Cyril Stegosaurus, and in the confusion, an AFC Fossil forward nipped in to score.

Terry told Cyril not to worry, it was only one goal. But from then on, it was all downhill for Terry and his team, and not just because their pitch sloped very steeply from one end to the other.

The team were five-nil down by half-time and most of their fans were already heading home.

Terry didn't dare look in the direction of his chairman.

Back in the dressing cave, Eric and Albert began fighting over who had the biggest half-time snack, while Terry tried to think of something positive to say about the team's performance.

WE GAVE AWAY MOST OF THOSE GOALS – THEY'RE NOT MAKING MANY OF THEIR OWN CHANCES.

"They don't need to," grumbled Steggy.

"We'll keep battling, boss," said Cyril, loyally, as the team trudged back onto the pitch. "Things can only get better."

Luckily, AFC Fossil were getting tired from having so many shots, so they didn't score *quite* as often in the second half. The game finished eight-nil. The crowd booed Dino FC off the pitch, and when Terry looked to see how Danny had reacted to the defeat, he saw his seat was already empty.

THAT'S NOT A GOOD SIGN.

Dino FC were now bottom of the table and there were only two games to go. Relegation was staring Terry and his team in the face like a big ugly tyrannosaurus!

Inside their dressing cave, Terry and the team were still sitting in their sweaty shirts. (Except for José Heterodontosaurus – with all his imaginary injuries, he never ran enough to get sweaty.)

Terry got to his feet and said he had something to tell them.

21

"To the bottom of the table," joked Archie Opteryx.

"You're not going to quit, are you?" said Gwen Corythosaurus, suddenly looking very worried. "Please don't go. You're a great manager! This is all our fault. We should have played better."

"But maybe his best's not good enough," growled a new voice. It was Dino FC chairman, Danny Deinonychus, who'd just entered the cave. His cruel teeth gleamed like the expensive rings on his claws.

Terry's heart sank. He felt sure that this was it – he was going to get the sack. He wished that he'd been given more time... time to bring in more of his own ideas. But now it looked like he would never get the chance.

AHEM, I HAVE AN IMPORTANT ANOUNCEMENT TO MAKE...

Danny, the BIG boss

Terry saw tears welling in Gwen's eyes.

"I'm going to make a change to the management team," continued Danny.

This was much too complicated for Marcus Diplodocus.

"What's wrong with the one you've got?" asked Marcus, still puzzled.

"Not a new face for *me*. A new face on the staff. I'm going to employ a fitness trainer."

"Who is this new trainer?" wondered Celia. "I hope it's someone famous." (Celia liked celebritysaurs and dreamed of being one herself some day.)

"His name," answered Danny, "is Hans Hadrosaur."

"No, he is not," continued Danny, "he's a very well respected trainer and he's going to lick you lot into shape. Starting tomorrow. Any objections?"

The team all turned to Terry. Surely he would never agree to this.

Terry knew that if Hans did well then he would probably get the manager's job, but Terry really wanted Dino FC to become a better team, and maybe – just maybe – Hans Hadrosaur could help. "What time do you want us at the ground?" he asked his chairman.

"Sunrise." Danny grinned.

Terry turned to Danny Deinonychus.
"We'll all be there at sunrise."

A very worried expression slowly crossed the faces of the entire squad as they realized that life as a Dino FC player was about to get a whole lot tougher.

Closer and closer to the edge of the jungle came the mystery runner, until the volcano-dotted plains beyond came into view.

"Hup three! Hup three! Hup three!"

A hand-painted sign pointed the way ahead: Dino FC training ground – 100 paces.

As Hans Hadrosaur looked at the sign, he continued jogging on the spot.

"Hup two! Hup two! Hup two..."

Hans was a squat, incredibly muscled dinosaur, with a firm jaw and dark, piercing eyes. He loved training and he loved making other people train. Peering ahead, he could just make out a football pitch and a set of goalposts made from palm trees.

"Now, to finish, Hans, one last sprint and no slacking!" (Hans Hadrosaur often talked to himself.)

"Onyourmarksgetsetgo!" he shouted and then sprinted flat out until he reached the tiny Dino FC training ground.

Everything was peaceful and calm. The first thing Hans saw was Archie Opteryx, fast asleep in the shade. The new trainer blew his whistle very loudly in Archie's ear.

The whistle was so loud that it not only woke Archie but also reached the rest of the team – from Pteradonna, dozing in her tree, to Gwen, bathing in the swamp, to Eric and Albert, fighting over what to have for breakfast.

Within minutes, Hans had assembled the squad on the training ground, and they found themselves running on the spot while he yelled at them in a deep throaty voice.

HUP TWO, HUP TWO, HUP TWO!
YOU HORRIBLE DINOSAURS...

"You've had it easy up to now, hup two, hup two, but those days are over. This is not a holiday camp, it's a sports ground, and I'm going to turn you wobbly-bottomed rabble into the fittest team in the dino-league, hup two, hup two – got that?!"

CHAPTER 5

Hans continued the team's training regime with what he called a "clinical assessment". These were big words for tiny dinosaur brains. Basically they meant that everyone had to get weighed and measured. Marcus Diplodocus was first onto the scales.

KERBONG! Marcus was so heavy that he crushed the scales and fell into the long grass.

"Just as I thought," growled the team's new trainer. "Out of shape."

Hans showed off his own muscles, which were as solid as Jurassic limestone. Even his muscles had muscles.

"Who's talking back?" snapped the trainer, angrily. "If anyone disagrees with my training methods they can leave the ground now...via the end of my boot!"

There was silence. It seemed Terry's team would rather keep training than face an angry Hans.

Even Terry took part, though he had tried very hard to get out of it.

ER, I'M NOT SURE I REALLY HAVE TIME TO GO FOR A RUN. I'VE GOT A LOT OF MANAGER STUFF TO DO...ER, PAPERWORK, PAINTING LINES ON THE PITCH, UM...

...MAYBE A FEW LAPS WOULDN'T HURT!

Fierce glower

Terry quickly hurried over to the grassy hillock where the rest of the squad were assembled.

"Twice round Mount Rumble!" barked Hans, blowing his whistle sharply.

"Twice!" grumbled José. "This is not a training run – it is like torture!"

"No pain, no gain," snarled Hans, who was able to run alongside the team without even getting out of breath. In fact he looked as if he could run all day.

Cyril Stegosaurus, on the other hand, didn't look that way at all. He was a slow moving plant-eater who usually only moved quickly if there was a pack of tyrannosauruses on his tail.

I CANNOT GO ON!

It was dark when the training session finally ended. "Tomorrow we'll concentrate on speed and strength work," growled Hans, and he jogged off into the sunset.

The team collapsed in a heap beneath the shadow of a giant ginkgo tree wondering if they'd ever be able to get up in the morning.

CHAPTER 6

Hans's terrifying training sessions continued all week, from dawn till dusk:

RUNNING UP AND DOWN VOLCANOES

LIFTING WEIGHTS

SWIMMING SWAMPS

There was no end to it! But even though he ached from his horns to the tip of his tail, Terry was pleased with the way things were progressing. Maybe it was his imagination, but the team looked much fitter. And where at first it had taken them all day to run round Mount Rumble, now they could do it in a few hours.

As the day of their next match dawned warm and sunny, Terry felt more hopeful than he'd done for a long time.

Rumbley Stadium was mostly empty, of course, with the regular fans joined only by a handful of supporters from their opponents, Carboniferous Limestone and Hove Albion. But it still felt like it was going to be a big day for Dino FC...the day they started to win matches!

Inside the dressing cave, Terry gave his prematch talk: "Thanks to Hans, we're fitter than we've ever been," he began, while the rest of the side pulled on their shirts or studied the team sheet. "Let's use our fitness and play at a high tempo with lots of movement!"

The team nodded. They liked feeling muscle where before there had been flab.

The ref now appeared and wished them all a good game.

Carboniferous Limestone and Hove Albion were already on the pitch warming up as Terry and his team trotted out.

Right from the kick-off, Dino FC went on the attack. Celia dribbled down the wing, whipped in a wicked cross and – WHUMPH – Eric Allosaurus powered a header into the back of the net. One-nil to Dino FC.

The training had paid off! Terry looked into the crowd and saw Hans Hadrosaur next to Danny Deinonychus. They both looked very pleased with themselves.

It had been some months since they'd last seen their team score. And even then it had been an own goal.

"I think this could be a turning point in Dino FC's season…" said football expert, Mark Megalosaurus.

But as often happens, the experts were wrong. It wasn't a turning point in Dino FC's season. In fact, things were about to go completely volcano-shaped!

Marcus Diplodocus was the first to run out of steam. He was just going to take a throw-in when he suddenly felt an overwhelming need to have a lie-down in the long grass. His legs felt as heavy as tree trunks. When Terry looked round to see what had happened to the throw-in, he was shocked to see his centre half fast asleep by the ball. Terry was too tired to be angry. In fact, he felt like having a nap himself.

FEELING WEARY...
MUST KEEP GOING...
YAWN...

Yawn

Elsewhere on the pitch it was the same story. The Dino FC players were moving in slow motion – like an action replay but without the action.

Carboniferous Limestone and Hove Albion could hardly believe their luck – it was like playing against a team of sleepwalkers.

And then they were awarded a penalty when midfielder Albert Allosaurus handled the ball while yawning.

Archie Opteryx was the liveliest player on the team, because he had missed a day's training to go to the dentist's, but even he was looking weary now.

The game ended ten-one to the Albion. Dino FC chairman, Danny Deinonychus, left the ground before the end, with a face like thunder. Terry guessed he wouldn't be the team's manager for much longer. Not unless he could conjure a win from somewhere. But where? And how?!

He had thought Danny's idea of using Hans as their trainer was a good one, but the plan had gone badly wrong. Looking at his exhausted team in the dressing cave, Terry knew he'd have to get Hans to leave. But that wasn't going to be easy. An angry looking Hans entered the room and blew his top like an out-of-control volcano.

"Well that was a disaster, wasn't it? You let me down, you let the fans down, you let the chairman down. You're still not fit enough, you bunch of weaklings! Time for another run!"

So while the Carboniferous Limestone and Hove Albion team relaxed in the aftermatch waterfall shower, Dino FC had to force their tired bodies on yet another run around Mount Rumble.

That night, Terry couldn't sleep for trying to think of a plan...

Next day Terry was pushing weights with the rest of the team when an idea hit him.

The only way to get rid of Hans was to get him a job somewhere else.

Danny Deinonychus had come to watch them training and still seemed to think that Hans "the Iron Dinosaur" was the best thing since flavoured lava.

DISCIPLINE! THAT'S WHAT THIS TEAM NEEDS. DISCIPLINE AND MORE LIFTING HEAVY THINGS!

Terry watched Hans and Danny talking and joking together and felt sure that the chairman wanted Hans as manager. He didn't have much time to save his job.

Meanwhile, Pteradonna had just finished 1,243 skips and was lying exhausted on the ground.

Terry knew he had to act fast before "the Iron Dinosaur" took over his team. But who could he find to offer Hans a job? Someone who wanted to spend their whole life lifting tree trunks and running round volcanoes?

There was only one place Terry could think of that fitted that description...

The head of the Macho-Dino Gym was a very fit ichthyostega called Indira. She read with interest the anonymous letter she'd just received, telling her all about a fantastic trainer called Hans Hadrosaur, the toughest trainer there had ever been, who might be available to come and work for her. There was also a picture of Hans, looking super-fit.

If you want someone who is as tough as a lump of volcanic rock, then I would recommend Hans. He is dedicated, loves his work, and is very good value for money. He also has his own whistle. I would definitely recommend you give him a job. ~~Please~~

Yours truly,
a well-wisher

The letter, of course, had come from Terry. He hoped that if Hans got a fantastic job offer from the exclusive gym, he might just take it.

Indira was very impressed with the sound of Hans Hadrosaur. But was she impressed enough to take him on?

Next morning, Hans Hadrosaur sprinted onto the training ground and told the team that he had an announcement to make.

More press-ups! thought Archie, wishing he was a million kilo-valleys away.

"He's going to make us run with weights on our tails," grumbled Marcus.

But what Hans had to say surprised everyone, except perhaps Terry.

"Today is our last session together," snapped Hans, running on the spot.

Terry thought this sounded hopeful.

AS FROM TOMORROW I WILL BE LEAVING TO TAKE UP A NEW POSITION AT A TOP GYM...

"I'll be working with great athletes, not mountains of blubber like you lot. And to celebrate my new position we'll be—"

"Doing double training," finished Hans, with a cruel smile. "Hup two! Hup two!"

But for once the team didn't mind the training. By tomorrow Hans would be gone and they could have a few days' rest before the final match of the season against Jurassic Park Rangers.

It was a game they really had to win. But of course Hans kept them running and weightlifting into the night, until it was darker than the inside of a velociraptor's jaws.

CHAPTER 10

With Hans finally gone, the team hoped
they would be able to relax and go back to
their old ways.

But they were about to be disappointed.
Terry might have thought Hans's training
routines were complete madness, but he
knew Hans had been right about some

WE'RE GOING TO KEEP ON TRAINING...

NOT MORE TRAINING.

things: the players weren't fit, and their old training sessions had been a shambles.

Terry shook his head. "No more of Hans's training methods. But we're not going to stop training altogether."

The team grumbled amongst themselves.

"In fact, we're going away on a team bonding exercise," continued Terry.

"Allosauruses don't bond," snarled Eric.

"Oh yes we do," growled back Albert, and they began to fight. Terry wondered if going away together was such a good idea after all. But the team needed to win their vital last game and Terry knew he needed to try something different.

CHAPTER 11

At first Terry was pleased with the way the bonding trip was going. He'd brought them to Triassic Bay, a remote seaside area where the weather was perfect and the food was fantastic. The team were getting on very well together, except for Eric and Albert, and even they weren't fighting as much as usual.

Terry took the team out on training runs; they swam in the sea; they talked about personal development programmes...

I WILL BE MORE POSITIVE.

I WILL NOT TEXT MY AGENT EVERY DAY TO ASK FOR TRANSFER.

Tired muscles started to recover. Gentle stretches and touching toes were the order of the day...

OOH, THAT'S A LONG WAY DOWN!

"We're in great shape, boss," grinned Cyril Stegosaurus, who in fact was quite a weird shape.

After heading practice, the team went out for a gentle jog. Suddenly, Archie Opteryx saw something he didn't like the look of one bit, and stopped dead in his tracks. The rest of the team collided into him one by one, forming a mini dinosaur-pile-up.

"That's up!" screamed Archie, pointing to an extremely fierce-looking tyrannosaurus lumbering towards them.

The tyrannosaurus opened its huge jaws and snarled… Its roar was so loud that the nearby trees were bent almost in two!

It was lucky Terry and his team had been training so hard or the tyrannosaurus would have caught them right away. They ran off as fast as they could, and up into a nearby forest. They hoped the tyrannosaurus wouldn't be able to follow them amongst the trees. But they were out of luck, because this tyrannosaurus was as nimble as a ballet dancer as it sprinted in and out of the greenery, with its razor-sharp claws outstretched and drool dripping from its teeth.

They could feel the swish of pursuing claws right behind them. Celia ran into a tree and flattened it to the ground. Archie leaped over a massive tree root and landed on Eric's tail. Suddenly, a huge ravine loomed up before the team...and the bad news was that it looked too wide to jump!

"I'll hold him up!" said Terry, bravely turning to face the tyrannosaurus. "The rest of you get going!"

Terry looked up at the huge meat-eating predator towering over him, and gave a deep gulp. He shouted back to the team.

Terry closed his eyes for what he thought would be the last time.

The tyrannosaurus licked its lips and reached out with a sharp and very scaly claw.

"Aren't you lot Dino FC?" he asked.

"Er, yes." Terry nodded.

"My dad used to support Dino FC. We lived near Rumbley Stadium until we had to move away after the big earthquake of sixty-six. We always look out for your results."

"They, er, haven't been very good recently," answered Terry, feeling ashamed of his team's recent performances.

BUT WE'LL BE GIVING IT OUR BEST SHOT.

"You need a win to stay up, don't you?" asked the young tyrannosaurus, as Terry signed his autograph book. Terry nodded. He was wondering where the rest of the team had fled to. Not too far away, he hoped. He didn't want them tired out again before the big match.

Luckily the others were quite close, hiding in the rim of an extinct volcano and listening to what was going on.

"Terry just risked his life for us," said Celia. "He faced that tyrannosaurus so we could get away."

WE OWE HIM ONE.

"You're right," added Celia. "We've got to pull together in the big match on Saturday and win it for Terry!"

It was Dino FC's last match of the season and the home crowd was bigger than usual. Everyone knew it was a huge match. Terry was glad to see so many extra faces... anything that could help lift the team's mood must be good, he figured. The maths was simple even for Marcus Diplodocus – Dino FC had to win, and then hope that their nearest rivals, Dynamo Dimetrodon, got beaten, otherwise they'd be relegated.

The team had been quiet inside the dressing cave and now, running out onto the pitch, they were still silent. Terry felt worried. His side was usually full of jokes and banter. He hoped nerves hadn't got to them.

"Dino FC! Dino FC!" chanted the crowd, sensing they could help. Today's match was against Jurassic Park Rangers, a good side who wouldn't be easily beaten.

The ref, a tiny eryops, blew his whistle and the game got under way. A long-range shot from Jurassic Park Rangers had Pteradonna flapping.

The shot hit the post, then the other post, and finally nestled in the back of the net.

Because they didn't want to let Terry down, Dino FC battled harder than they'd done all season. Jurassic Park Rangers were hanging on by their claws.

The ref blew the whistle for half-time!

Terry didn't have to give his usual half-time talk. The rest of the team were determined to do their best for him and started coming up with ideas of their own.

"Let's push Steggy into midfield," suggested Gwen.

"And let's look to get Celia in down the left," added Cyril, who'd never had an idea about tactics before in his life.

"Enough talk — let's go get 'em," snarled Albert. "This team ain't going down!"

Forty-five minutes to save Dino FC from defeat! The second half began with them on the attack. Attracted by the noise from the ground, a few more locals had swelled the crowd and were now urging the team on.

There was a corner from the right-hand bush. Archie struck it sweet as a nut, an inswinger with plenty of pace. As it swooped towards the crossbar, a couple of Jurassic

players leaped for it and missed. But Steggy
didn't. His extra-strong skull met the ball
and rocketed it into the back of the net.

With Steggy now in midfield and the
Allosaurus brothers tackling the opposition

instead of each other, Dino FC had Jurassic penned back into their own half. Even Terry, a defender, was joining in the attacks. He played a one-two with Cyril, who couldn't count any higher than two, and chipped a teasing ball into the box. Celia dummied and it ran through to José Heterodontosaurus. He chested the ball down and hit a screaming volley into the top of the net.

83

Two-one! As the sun slowly began to set behind the trees, Dino FC were in the lead and only ten minutes remained. They would be ten very long minutes...

Jurassic Park were awarded a free kick after Eric bit a piece out of the corner bush.

They took it quickly, before Terry had time to organize a defensive wall, and a shot flew towards Dino FC's goal. The ball swerved like a dragonfly in a hurricane.

Pteradonna took off and, with claws outstretched, pushed the shot over the bar.

"What a save!" said Mark Megalosaurus up in the DBC commentary box.

"The best since my own save against Inter Diplodocus five years ago," agreed Gary Seymouria, who was a bit of a big-head.

That shot was Jurassic Park's last chance of the match. Dino FC had held on to win two-one! But still they couldn't celebrate. Not yet. They needed to know the result from the other match.

After a nervous wait, a dragonfly
brought them the news.

VOLCANO VALLEY TWO...
DYNAMO DIMETRODON NIL.

Terry raised his arms in triumph!

Dynamo Dimetrodon were relegated
and Dino FC had stayed in the Dino
Premiership by the skin of their teeth. Now
the team could finally celebrate!

As they ran round the pitch, performing their lap of honour, Terry pulled Celia to one side. "What happened today? I don't understand why you all played so brilliantly."

Celia smiled as she signed an autograph for a young fan.

IT WAS BECAUSE WE SAW YOU FACE THAT TYRANNOSAURUS ALONE.

BUT HE WAS JUST A FAN.

"Yes, but you didn't know that. You were prepared to risk your life for us. So we figured the best way to say thanks was to try and play better than we've ever played in our lives!"

"You sure did that!" Terry smiled, feeling very proud of his team. He had a feeling next season was going to be a whole lot more fun than this one had been.

"We might even win a trophy," thought Terry to himself, as he made his way from the ground, cheered all the way by fans and teammates. He had rediscovered his love of football, and was already planning tactics for the pre-season games!

WE'RE GOING TO ATTACK MORE... AND SCORE LOTS OF GOALS... AND I MIGHT EVEN PLAY FOUR UP FRONT. OH, IT'S GOING TO BE GREAT!!!

THE END

MEET THE PLAYERS IN DINO FC

- THE CRAZIEST TEAM IN THE JURASSIC WORLD!

RUMBLEY STADIUM - THE DINO FC GROUND

PTERADONNA 1

POSITION: goalkeeper
SKILLS: flying
LIKES: catching crosses
DISLIKES: non-football days
FOOTY FACT: the youngest member of the squad

STEGGY STEGOCERAS 2

POSITION: defender
SKILLS: good at marking opponents
LIKES: grumbling
DISLIKES: being told what to do
FOOTY FACT: applied for the manager's job but Terry got it

MARCUS DIPLODOCUS 3

POSITION: defender
SKILLS: great in the air
LIKES: heading the ball
DISLIKES: quick forwards
FOOTY FACT: last season won 76% of all headers

TERRY TRICERATOPS 4

POSITION: manager and fullback
SKILLS: tactician
LIKES: tough talking
DISLIKES: defensive football
FOOTY FACT: only player-manager in the DPL

CYRIL STEGOSAURUS — 5

POSITION: fullback
SKILLS: following instructions
LIKES: moving slowly
DISLIKES: anyone criticizing Terry, "the boss"
FOOTY FACT: the vice-captain

ALBERT ALLOSAURUS — 6

POSITION: midfield
SKILLS: dealing with tricky forwards
LIKES: arguing with his twin
DISLIKES: Eric. Refs
FOOTY FACT: once got 21 red cards in a season

GWEN CORYTHOSAURUS — 7

POSITION: midfield
SKILLS: controlling midfield
LIKES: playing in the rain
DISLIKES: hot temperatures
FOOTY FACT: the team's free kick specialist

ARCHIE OPTERYX — 8

POSITION: winger
SKILLS: great dribbler
LIKES: doing ball tricks
DISLIKES: bumpy pitches
FOOTY FACT: takes the team's corners

ERIC ALLOSAURUS — 9

POSITION: **midfield**
SKILLS: **tackling, marking**
LIKES: **arguing with his twin**
DISLIKES: **Albert. Refs**
FOOTY FACT: **once got 20 red cards in a season**

CELIA COELOPHYSIS — 10

POSITION: **forward**
SKILLS: **fast and graceful**
LIKES: **looking good on the pitch**
DISLIKES: **tackling or being tackled**
FOOTY FACT: **fastest player on the team**

JOSÉ HETERODONTOSAURUS — 11

POSITION: **forward**
SKILLS: **falling over in the box**
LIKES: **winning penalities**
DISLIKES: **most things**
FOOTY FACT: **on average only fit for 2.3 games per season**

OLLIE OVIRAPTOR — 12

POSITION: **utility player**
SKILLS: **football brain, experience**
LIKES: **resting after the match**
DISLIKES: **playing 90 minutes**
FOOTY FACT: **has been a pro for 22 seasons**

CHECK OUT MORE CRAZY FOOTY ACTION IN:

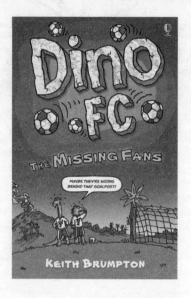

Dino FC never had many fans.
Now, even those fans have deserted them
so the club's strapped for cash – and Terry
wants to buy a new striker...

ISBN 9781409504849

Coming soon...
THE GREAT KIT CATASTROPHE
THE VANISHING GOALIE

For more action-packed reads head to